WHERE THE WILD THINGS ARE

WHERE THE WILD THINGS ARE

STORY AND PICTURES BY MAURICE SENDAK

HARPER COLLINS PUBLISHERS

The night Max wore his wolf suit and made mischief of one kind

and another

his mother called him "WILD THING!"
and Max said "I'LL EAT YOU UP!"
so he was sent to bed without eating anything.

That very night in Max's room a forest grew

and grew—

and grew until his ceiling hung with vines
and the walls became the world all around

and an ocean tumbled by with a private boat for Max
and he sailed off through night and day

and in and out of weeks
and almost over a year
to where the wild things are.

And when he came to the place where the wild things are
they roared their terrible roars and gnashed their terrible teeth

and rolled their terrible eyes and showed their terrible claws

till Max said "BE STILL!"
and tamed them with the magic trick

of staring into all their yellow eyes without blinking once
and they were frightened and called him the most wild thing of all

and made him king of all wild things.

"And now," cried Max, "let the wild rumpus start!"

"Now stop!" Max said and sent the wild things off to bed without their supper. And Max the king of all wild things was lonely and wanted to be where someone loved him best of all.

Then all around from far away across the world
he smelled good things to eat
so he gave up being king of where the wild things are.

But the wild things cried, "Oh please don't go—
we'll eat you up—we love you so!"
And Max said, "No!"

The wild things roared their terrible roars and gnashed their terrible teeth
and rolled their terrible eyes and showed their terrible claws
but Max stepped into his private boat and waved good-bye

and sailed back over a year
and in and out of weeks
and through a day

and into the night of his very own room
where he found his supper waiting for him

and it was still hot.

THE CROW KING

This edition published by Mantra Lingua Ltd,
Global House, 303 Ballards Lane, London N12 8NP, UK
www.mantralingua.com

Karga Kral

Bir Kore Halk Hikayesi

The Crow King

A Korean Folk Story

by Lee Joo-Hye
Illustrated by Han Byung-Ho
Retold in English by Enebor Attard

Turkish translation by Talin Altun Suzme

Uzun zaman önce, kargaların ülkesinde, korku ile yöneten bir kral yaşardı.
İstediği herkesi alırdı ve kimse de onu durduramazdı.
Bir gün, bir kadın ve bir adam eve giderken Karga Kral geldi.
Hızla uçarak kadını pençelerinin arasında yakaladı ve kimsenin asla
gitmediği dağların dik yamaçlarına götürdü.

A long time ago, in the land of the crows, there lived a king who ruled with terror.
He would take anyone he liked and no-one could stop him.
One day, a man and woman were going home when the Crow King came.
In one giant swoop he grabbed the woman and flew away to the steep and
lofty peaks where no human had ever been.

Beyaz sislerin arasından görmese de, toprak yıpratıcı ve karanlık olsa da,
adam kadını bulmaya yemin etti.

The man swore that he would find the woman even though the land was rough
and gloomy, and he could barely see through the white mist.

Adam yükseklere tırmandı ve sonunda bir münzevinin yaşadığı kulübeye geldi.
"Daha fazla ilerleme," diye onu uyardı münzevi. "Senden önce çok deneyenler oldu."
Adam korkmadığını, sevgisinin gerçek olduğunu söyledi.
"Genç adam, güçlü olmak için cesarete ihtiyacın var," dedi münzevi. "Onu bulmak için oniki tane kapı açman gerekecek, ve her bir kapının arkasında kargalar seni öldürmek için bekliyor olacak! Unutma ki ne olursa olsun, kötülüğün bile bir sonu vardır." Sonra, içeriden pirinçten yapılmış kekler getirerek, "Kargaları yenmek için bunları al," dedi.

He climbed higher and higher until he came to a hut where a hermit lived.
"Go no further," she warned. "Many have tried before you."
The man said he was not frightened, for his love was true.
"Young man, you will need courage to be strong," the hermit said. "Twelve doors must you open to find her and at each door the crows watch, waiting to kill you! Remember, no matter what happens, even evil has an end." Then, bringing some rice cakes from her hut, she said, "Here, take these to trick the crows."

Rüzgar daha da kuvvetli esti, yağmur daha da fazla yağdı. O kadar karanlıktı ki adam gökyüzünün düştüğünü sandı. Adam adım adım ilerledi ve sonunda oniki tane kapısı ve heryerde uçan, gagalayan, ciyaklayan, seyreden – ilerideki tehlikeyi görmezden gelen adamı seyreden – kargalar olan kaleye geldi.

The winds blew wilder, the rain fell harder. It was so dark that the man thought the sky had fallen down. Step by step the man climbed until he saw the fortress of a dozen doors with crows everywhere - flying, pecking, screeching, watching - watching this foolish man ignore the danger ahead.

İlk kapıda adam kargalara pirinçten yapılmış keki gösterdi ve uzağa fırlattı.
Karagalar ona aldırmadan keke uçuştu. Adam sessizce ikinci kapıdan geçti.
Aynı şeyi her seferinde tekrarladı ve her seferinde de kargalar ona aldırmadı.

At the first door the man showed the crows one rice cake and flung it far away.
The birds ignored him and rushed to the cake while the man quietly slipped through to the
second door. He did this over and over again and each time the crows ignored him.

Onikinci kapıyı açınca adam bir gölün ortasında bir ev gördü.
Kadına seslendi ve o da koşarak sevinç içinde adama sarıldı.
"Acele et," dedi, "canavar Karga Kral birazdan gelecek."

Opening the twelfth door the man saw a house in the middle of a lake.
He called to the woman who rushed out and hugged him with joy.
"Hurry," she said, "the monster Crow King will be back very soon."

İçeride ejderha saplı bir kılıç ve bir çift ayakkabı vardı.
"Çabuk," dedi kadın, "bunlar canavarın ve sen almalısın."
Ama kılıç fazla ağırdı ve ayakkabılar da fazla büyük.
Kadın bir sürahiye gölden su doldurarak adama verdi ve,
"Bunu iç, sana cesaret verir," dedi.

Inside was a huge sword with a dragon handle and a pair of shoes.
"Quick," she said, "these belong to the monster and you must take them."
But the sword was too heavy and the shoes were too big.
Filling a jug with water from the lake, the woman cried, "Drink this tonic,
it will give you courage."

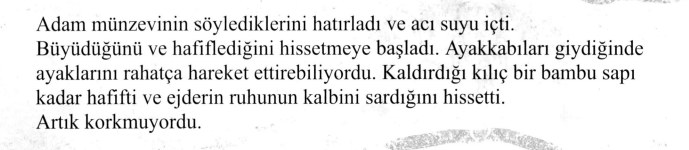

Adam münzevinin söylediklerini hatırladı ve acı suyu içti.
Büyüdüğünü ve hafiflediğini hissetmeye başladı. Ayakkabıları giydiğinde
ayaklarını rahatça hareket ettirebiliyordu. Kaldırdığı kılıç bir bambu sapı
kadar hafifti ve ejderin ruhunun kalbini sardığını hissetti.
Artık korkmuyordu.

The man recalled what the hermit said and drank the bitter liquid.
He could feel himself growing bigger and lighter. He put on the shoes
and his feet danced and kicked with ease. The sword he lifted was
as light as a bamboo branch and he felt the spirit of the dragon
enter his heart.
He was not afraid.

Kısa bir süre sonra geldiler. Önce Karga Kral ve arkasından ciyaklayıp tükürerek taraftar kargalar.

They came a moment later. First the Crow King, then his follower crows, shrieking and spitting.